3-14

D0116124

TWO BUNNY BUDDIES

Kathryn O. Galbraith

Illustrated by Joe Cepeda

Houghton Mifflin Harcourt
Boston • New York

For two special buddies, Emma and Jake. And for my special buddy, Steve —K.O.G.

For Isabella and Mayali, two cute bunnies —J.C.

Text copyright © 2014 by Kathryn O. Galbraith
Illustrations copyright © 2014 by Cepeda Studio Inc.

All rights reserved. For information about permission to reproduce selections from this book, write to Permissions,
Houghton Mifflin Harcourt Publishing Company, 215 Park Avenue South, New York, New York 10003.

www.hmhbooks.com

The text type was set in Tokig Px.

Library of Congress Cataloging-in-Publication Data
Galbraith, Kathryn Osebold.
Two bunny buddies / Kathryn O. Galbraith ; Illustrated by Joe Cepeda.
pages cm
Summary: On their way to have lunch together, two friends have an argument, but when they go their separate ways, each misses his buddy.
ISBN 978-0-544-17652-2
[1. Friendship—Fiction. 2. Rabbits—Fiction.] I. Cepeda, Joe, illustrator. II. Title.
PZ7.G1303Two 2014   [E]—dc23   2013020192

Manufactured in China
SCP 10 9 8 7 6 5 4 3 2 1

4500447607

Two bunny buddies, hungry for lunch.

The sun is hot.
The path is long.

"Let's go that way."

"Stinky Feet! Jump, jump this way!"

"Birdy Breath! Hop, hop that way!"

One bunny here.

One bunny there.

"Look!"
Berries, red and ripe.
But there is no buddy to look.

"See!"
Clover, green and sweet.
But there is no buddy to see.

One bunny sighs.

One bunny cries.

Quick, quick!
Pick berries,
red and ripe.

Hurry, hurry!
Gather clover,
green and sweet.

The sun is hot.

The paths are long.

Jump,   jump,   jump.

Hop, hop, hop.

"Hello, buddy!"

"Hello, buddy!"

Two bunny buddies
nibble and munch.

Yum. Yum. Yum.
One delicious lunch.